I Can Draw
MONSTERS

by Tony Tallarico

Little Simon

THIS BOOK IS DEDICATED TO—
Dr. Frankenstein, Blob, Count Dracula,
Werewolf, Mummy, Boris Karloff, Bram Stoker,
Dr. Jekyll and Mr. Hyde, Nina, Anthony, Elvira,

and most of all to you _____.

LITTLE SIMON
Copyright © 1981 by Anthony Tallarico
An imprint of Simon & Schuster Children's Publishing Division
1230 Avenue of the Americas
New York, New York 10020
All rights reserved including the right of reproduction
in whole or in part in any form.
LITTLE SIMON and colophon are trademarks of Simon & Schuster.
ISBN: 0-689-81196-9
10 9 8 7 6 5 4 3 2

You'll have fun
turning odd
shapes...

1

into odd
looking
monsters.

2

MR. OOZE

The first five steps should be drawn lightly in pencil. Don't be surprised if you have to erase a lot, but make your corrections and additions before erasing.

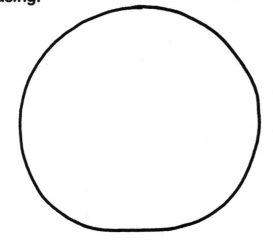

1

Draw a not too
perfect circle.

2

Divide it into
quarters.

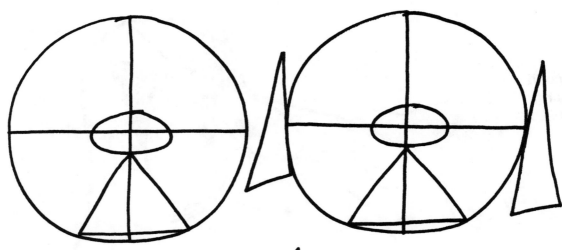

3

Add an oval shape
in the center
and a triangle
under it.

4

Add two more
triangles.

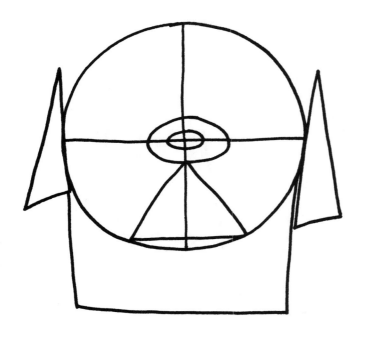

5

Draw another oval
in the center,
and box off
your drawing
on the bottom.

6

Complete
the monster
by adding
your own details,
or follow the
ones here.

ONE EYE

Draw the first five steps lightly in pencil.

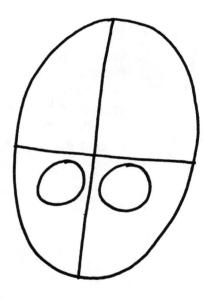

1

First draw an
egg shape.

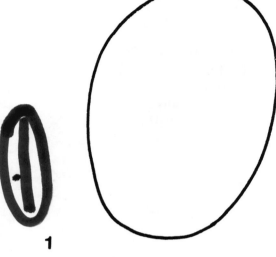

2

Now cut the
shape in half.

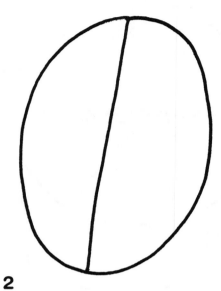

3

Cut it in half
again and add
two circles.

4

Add another circle
and two
upside-down triangles.

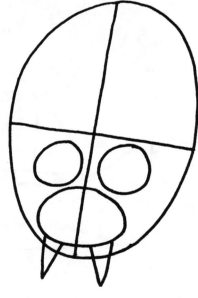

5

Add two more
ovals and two
half-moon shapes.

6

Add some details,
as shown,
to complete
your monster and...
RUN FOR YOUR LIFE!

HORNED THING

Draw the first four steps lightly in pencil.

1

2

3

4

Use your
imagination to
make the monster
more monstrous.

5

THE BLAH

Draw the first five steps lightly in pencil.

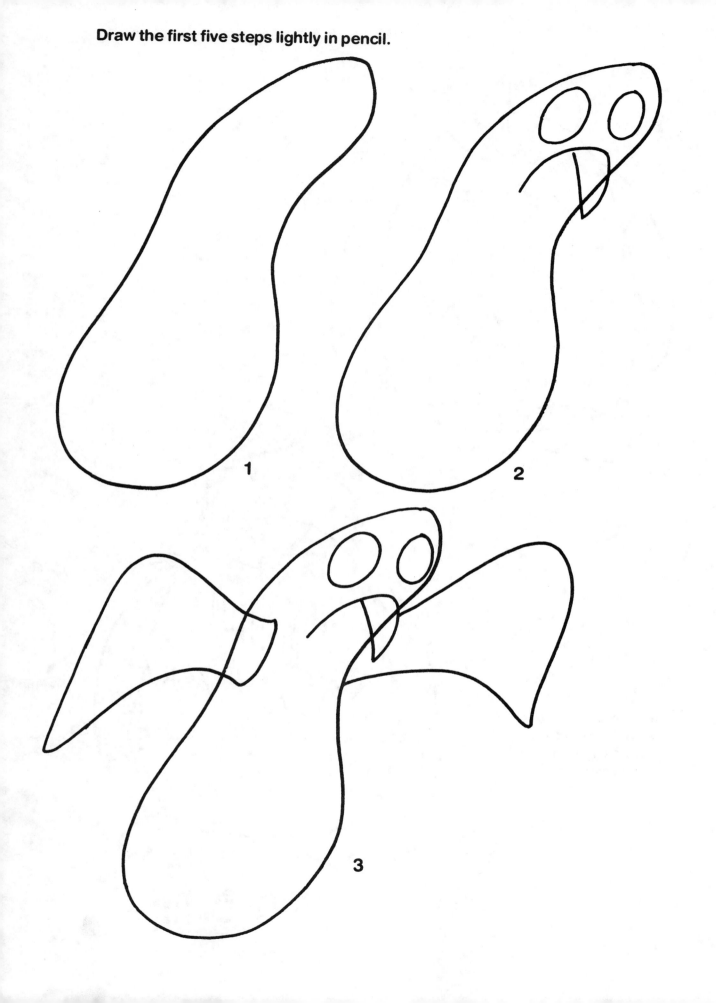

4

WINGED GHOUL

5

Add your own
ghoulish
finishing touches
to the monster.

Draw the first four steps lightly in pencil.

1

2

3

4

SPOTS

STITCHES

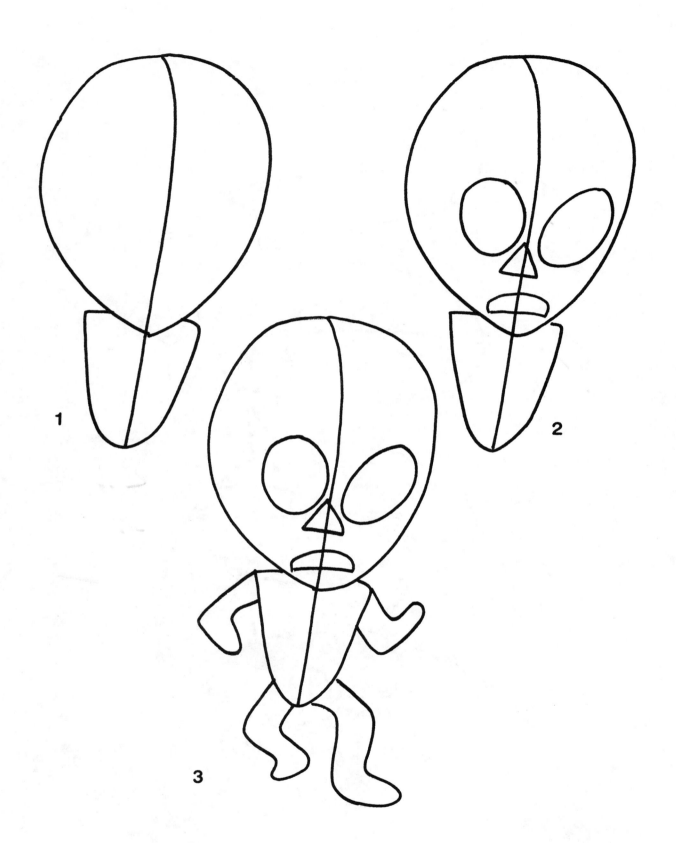

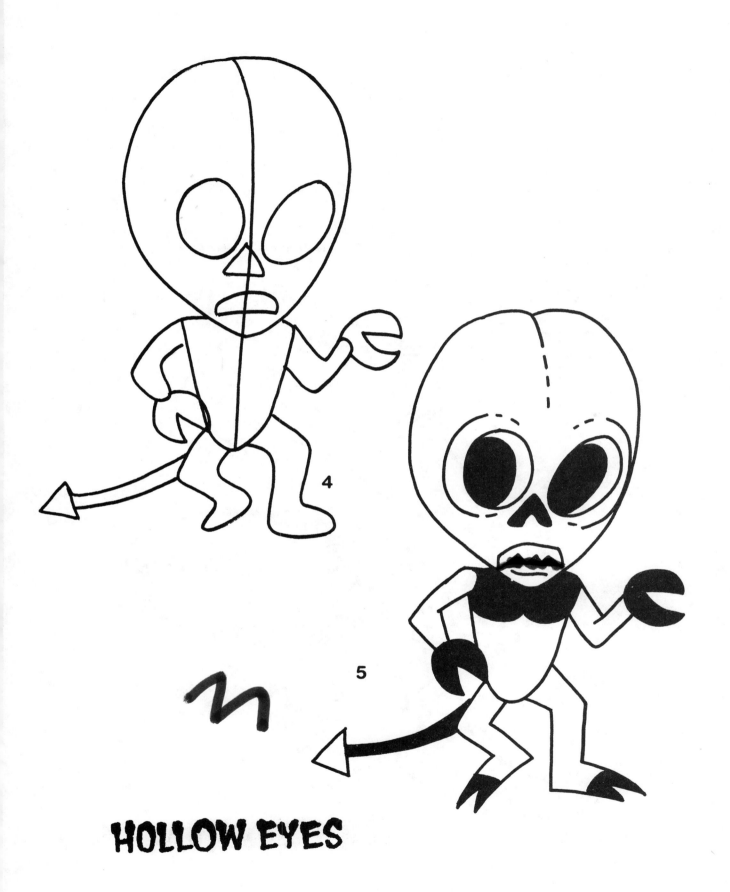

4

5

HOLLOW EYES

1

2

3

THE SQUIRM

1

2

3

4

DRAGONETTE

1

2

3

4

ELVIRA THE WITCH

1

2

3

4

GLOP

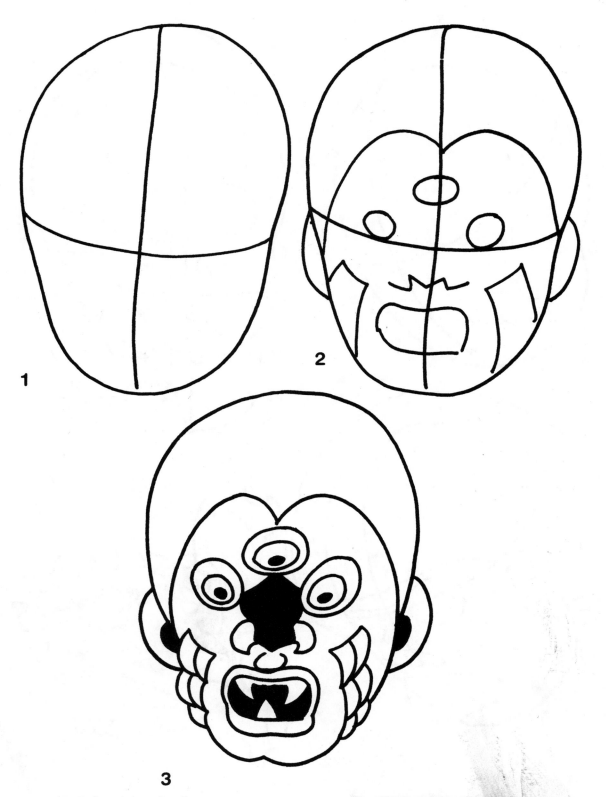

1

2

3

TRI-EYES

1

2

3

MELVIN

1

2

3

4

SQUINT

1

2

3

SPIKE

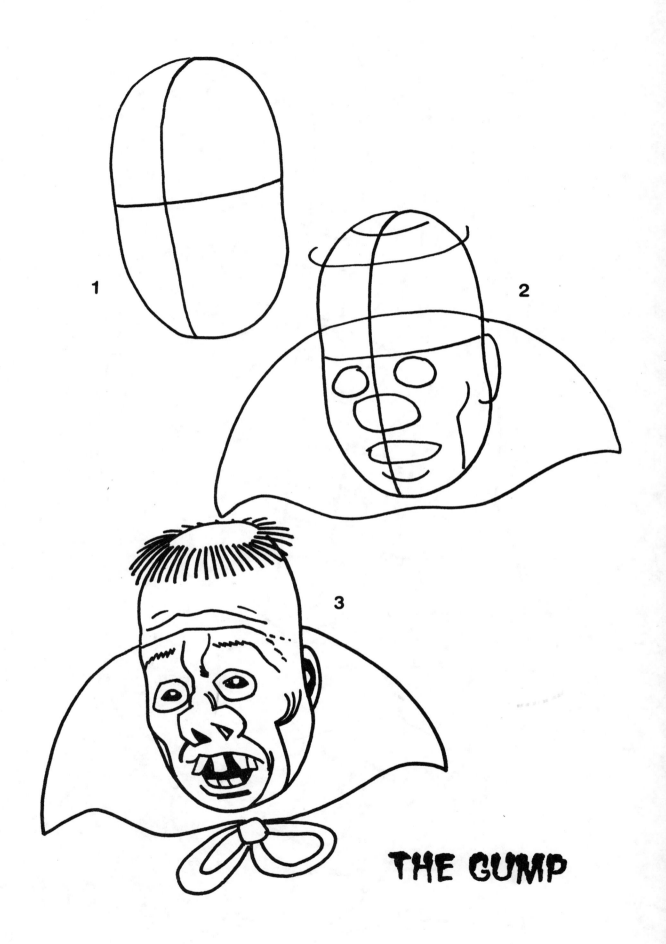

1

2

3

THE GUMP

1

2

3

4

GALLAX

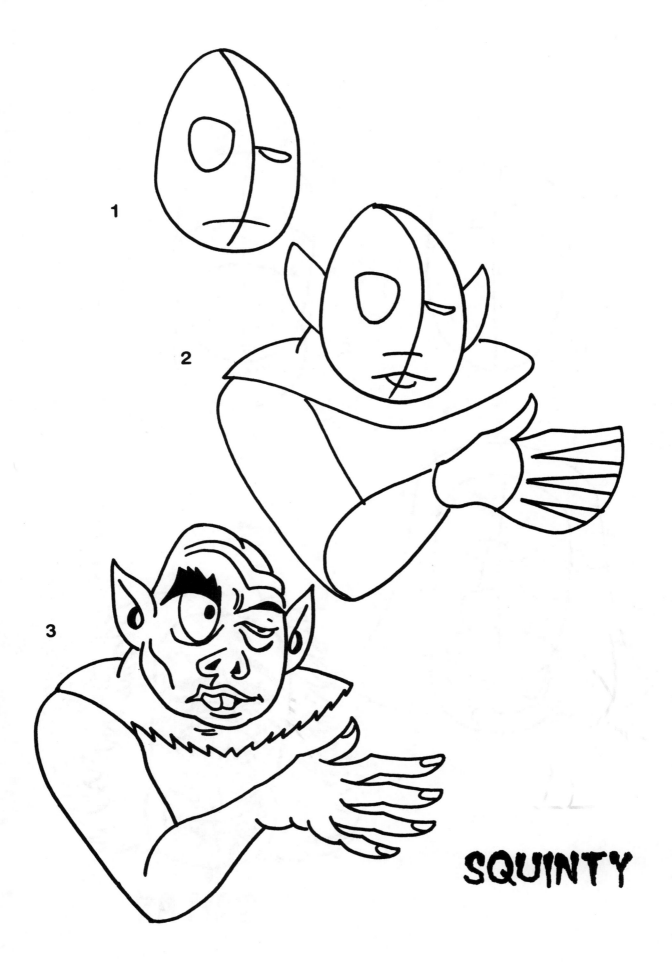

1

2

3

SQUINTY

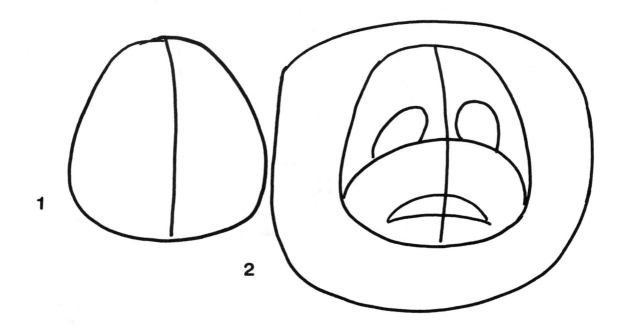

1

2

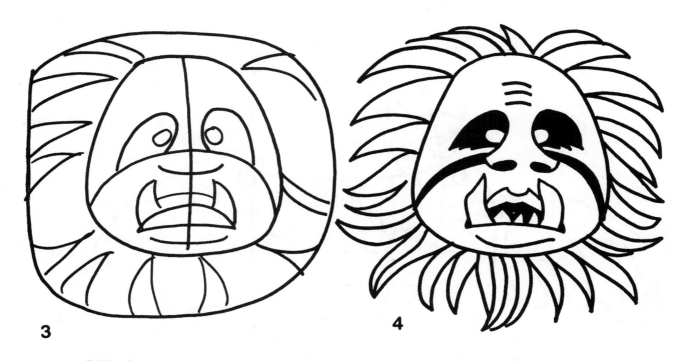

3

4

TOOLANG

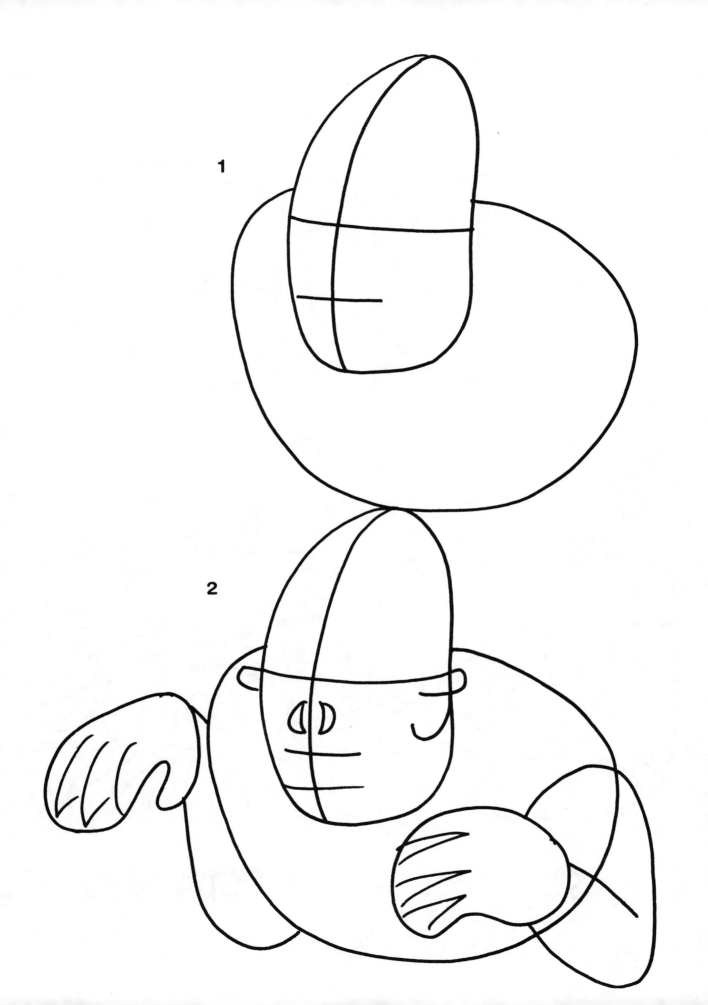

SUBTERRANEAN BEING

1

2

3

RUBA

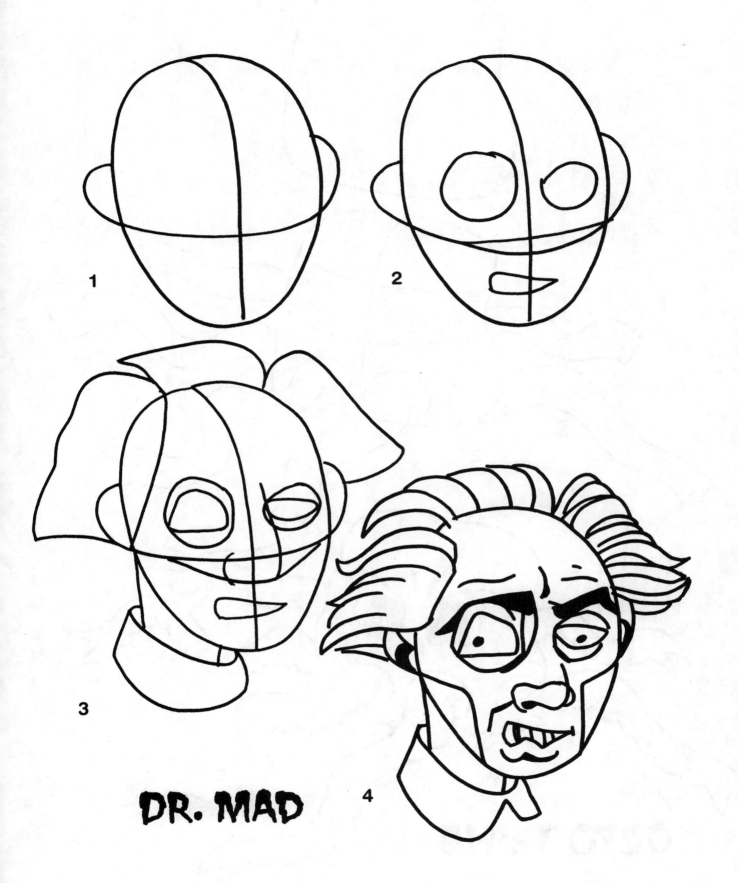

1

2

3

DR. MAD

4

1

2

3

OCTO-THING

1

2

3

THE ALIEN

1

2

3

GIANT GORE

FLY

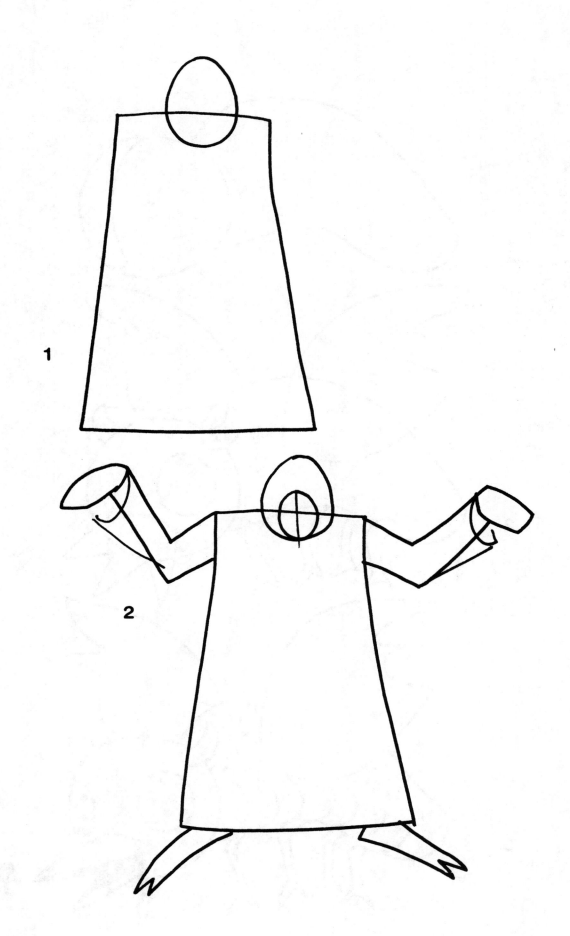

3

GHOSTLY SKULL

1

2

3

BIG FOOT

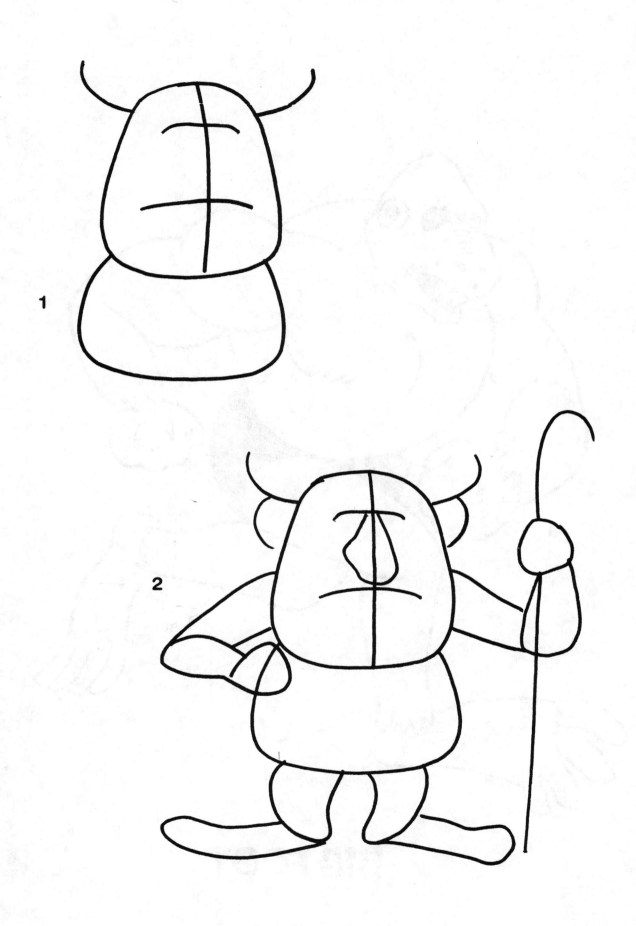

3

THE EVIL DWARF

1

2

3

KILLER BAT

1

2

3

EFUS

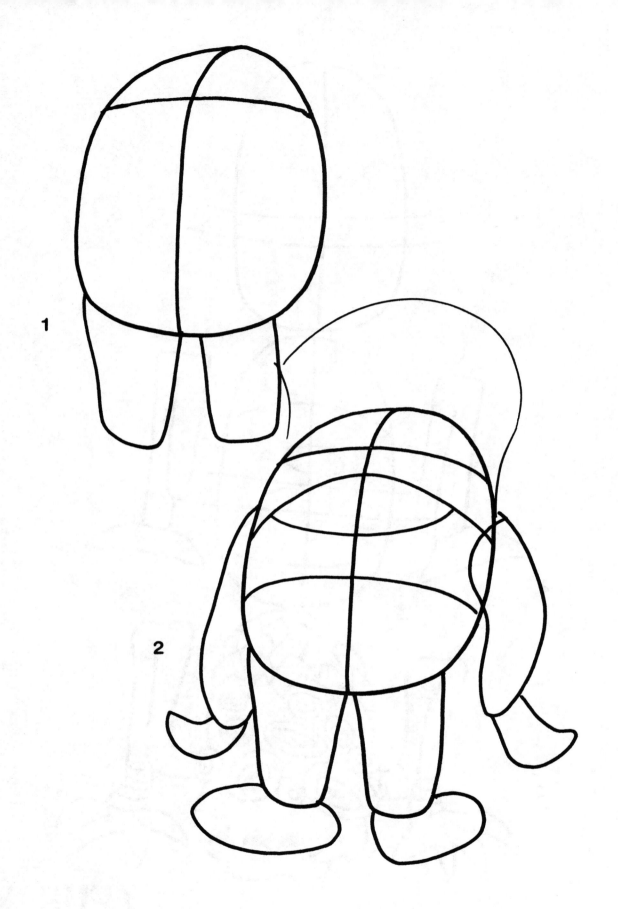

3

HORNED MOLE

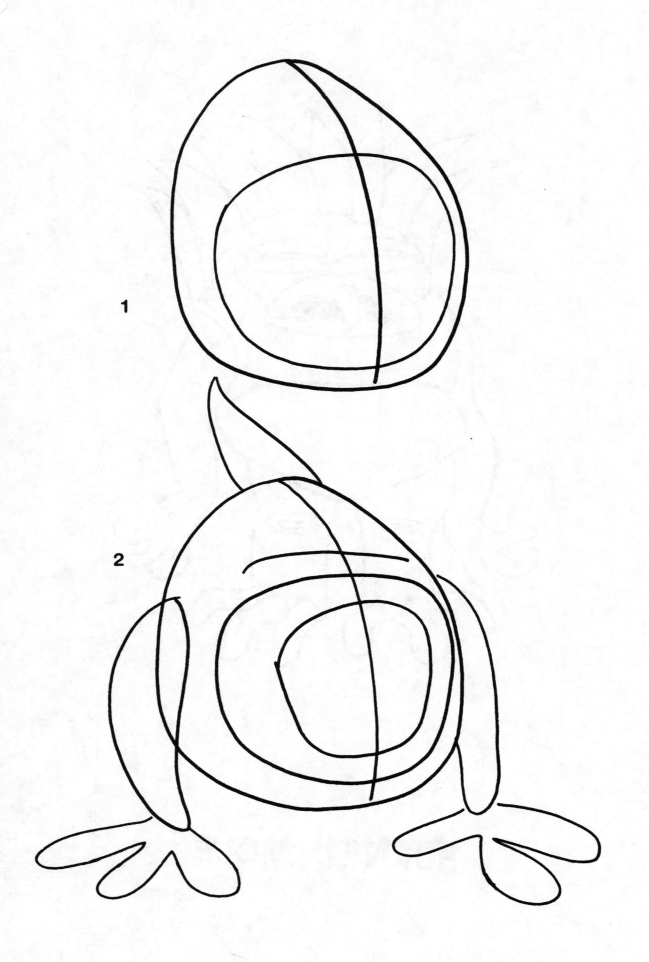

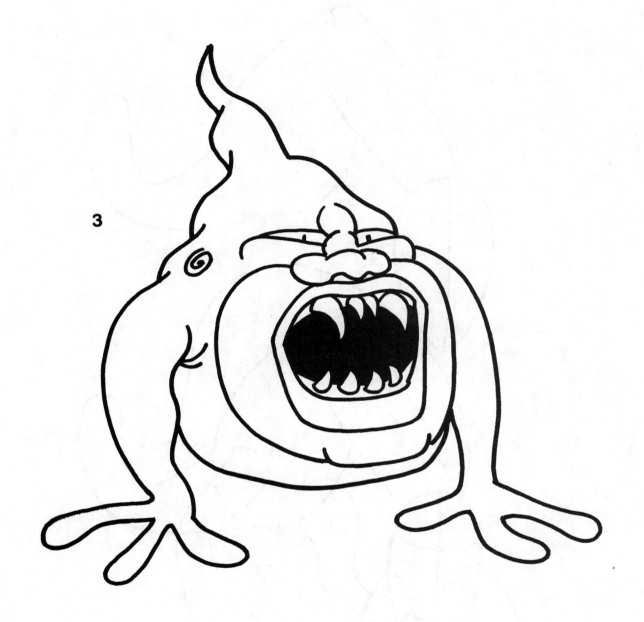

3

BARTOK, THE MOLD

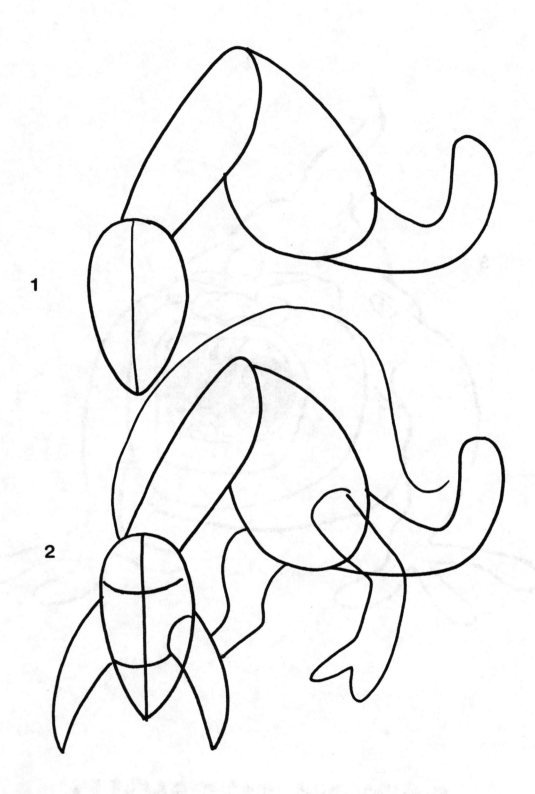

3

BIG-TOOTHED DRAGON

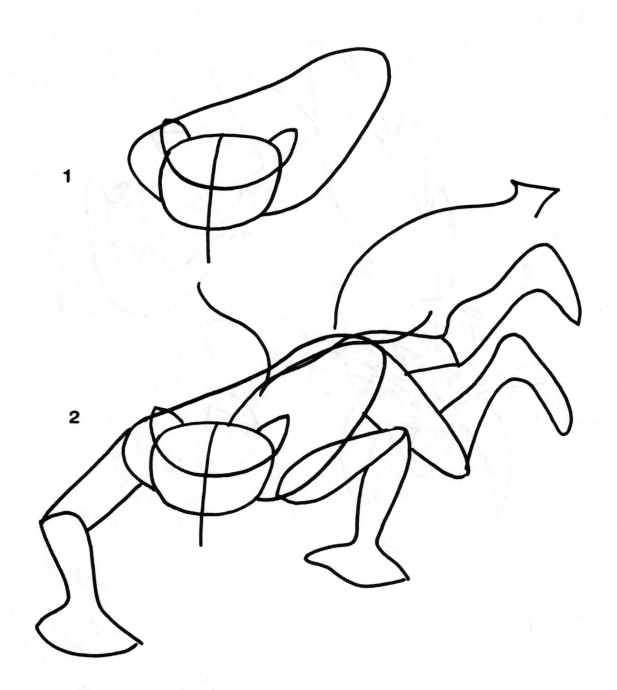

3

WINGED DEVIL

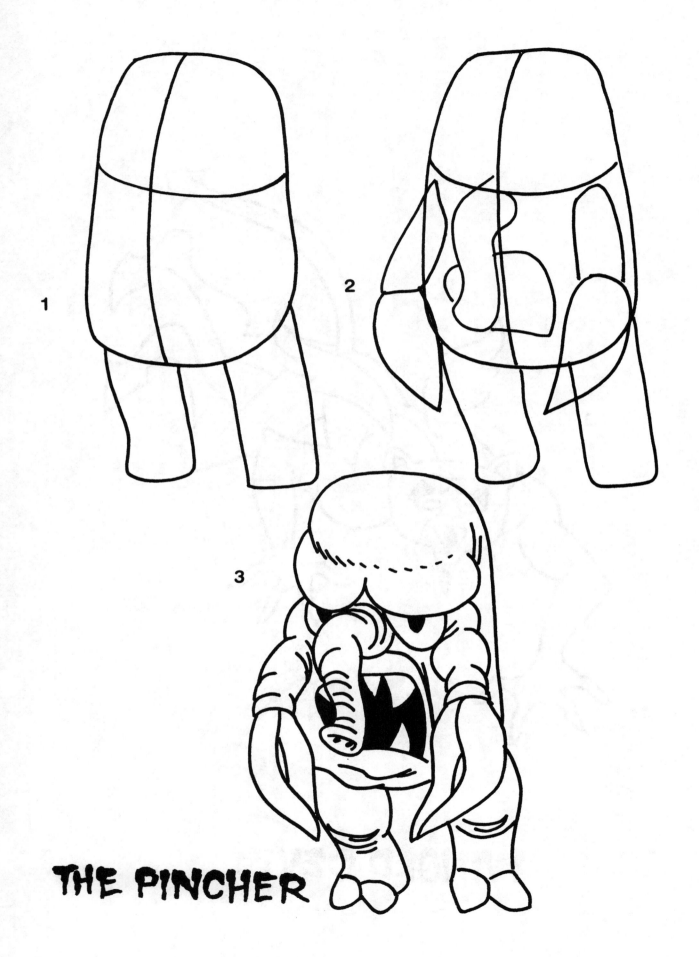

1

2

3

THE PINCHER

1

2

3

MOLT

1

2

WEREWOLF

1

2

3

HAIRY

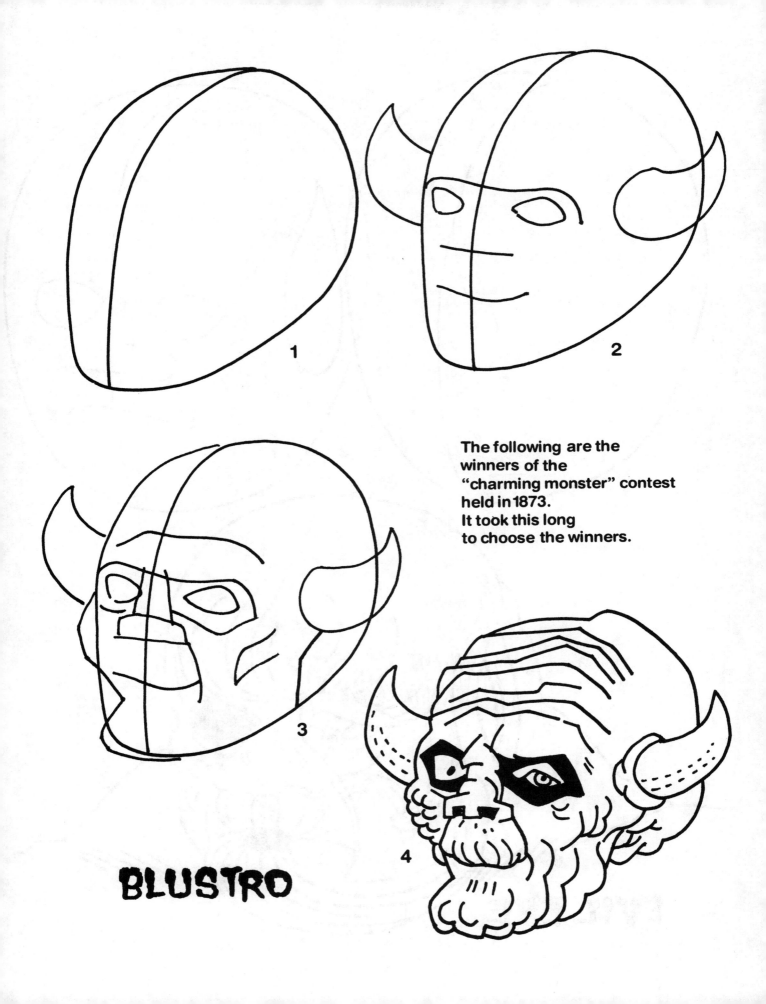

1

2

3

The following are the
winners of the
"charming monster" contest
held in 1873.
It took this long
to choose the winners.

4

BLUSTRO

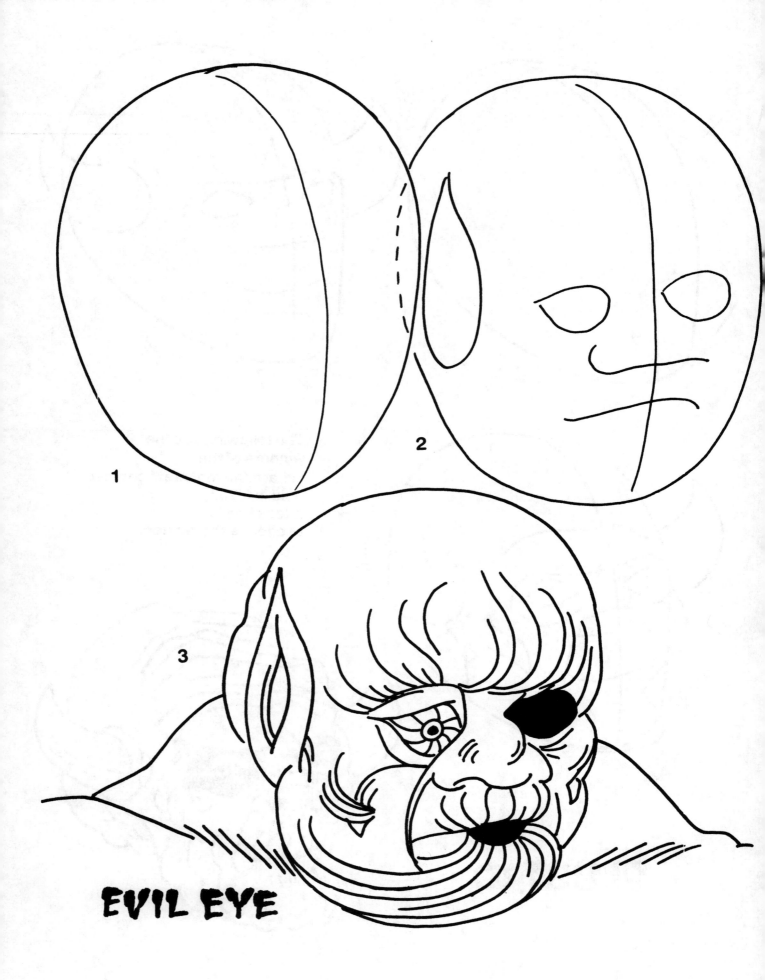

EVIL EYE

1

2

3

GOATEE

1

2

3

GORE

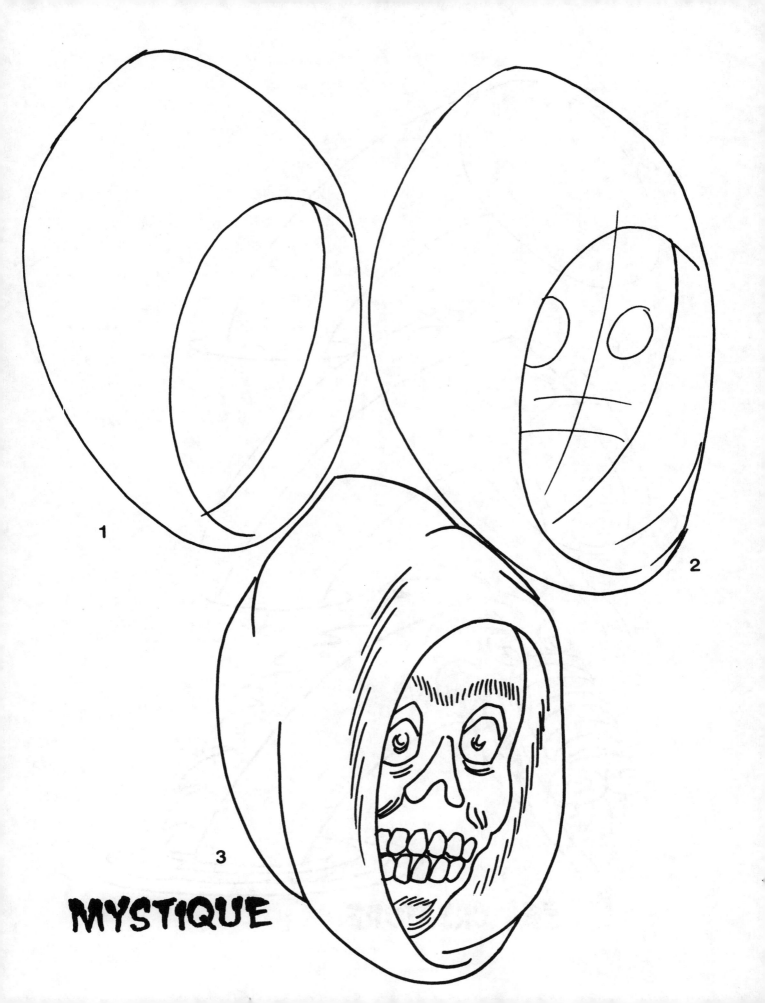

1

2

3

MYSTIQUE

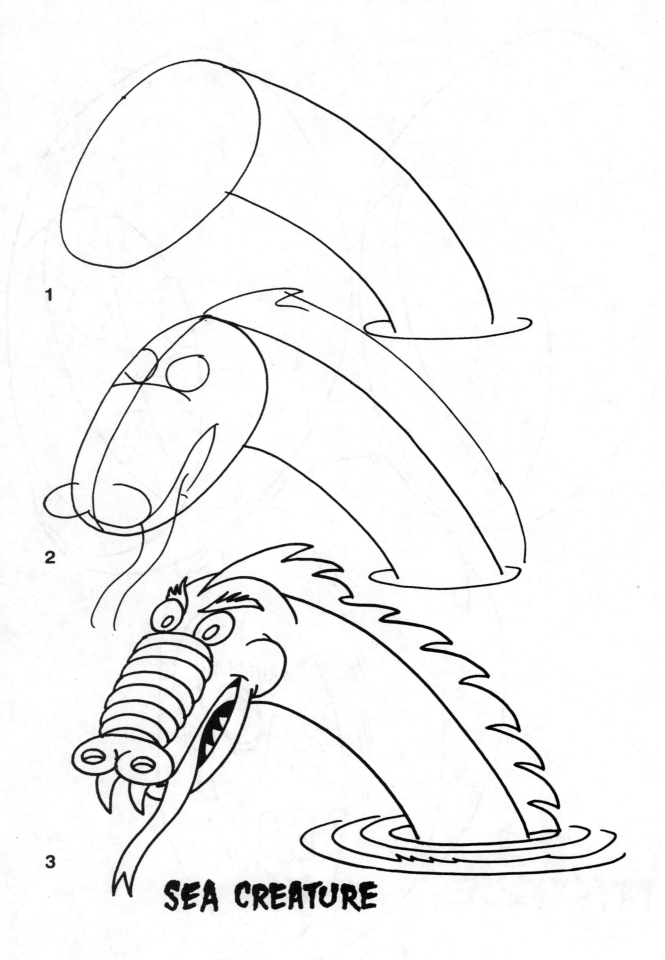

1

2

3

SEA CREATURE